PUFFIN

HARVEY

When a meteor knocks Ace Space pilot Harvey and his animal crew across the galaxy, things don't look good. Then their spaceship, ARK 1, lands on Phungos V and things begin to look worse – much worse. Not only is Phungos V one vast junk-heap, it is also ruled by the most slovenly amateur Space Baddie in the cosmos – Ozalid Crust!

Find out how a 'Paradise Planet' got into such a mess and discover Ozalid Crust's secret dream in this crazy spacy story!

Robin Kingsland was born in Bristol and now lives in London. When he is not writing and illustrating, Robin is acting. He is married to Fiona and has two cats. He has had several books published but this is his first in Young Puffin.

Harvey's Ark

Written and illustrated by
ROBIN KINGSLAND

PUFFIN BOOKS

PUFFIN BOOKS

Published by the Penguin Group
Penguin Books Ltd, 27 Wrights Lane, London W8 5TZ, England
Penguin Books USA Inc., 375 Hudson Street, New York, New York 10014, USA
Penguin Books Australia Ltd, Ringwood, Victoria, Australia
Penguin Books Canada Ltd, 10 Alcorn Avenue, Toronto, Ontario, Canada M4V 3B2
Penguin Books (NZ) Ltd, 182–190 Wairau Road, Auckland 10, New Zealand

Penguin Books Ltd, Registered Offices: Harmondsworth, Middlesex, England

First published by Hamish Hamilton Ltd 1990
Published in Puffin Books 1992
1 3 5 7 9 10 8 6 4 2

Printed in England by Clays Ltd, St Ives plc

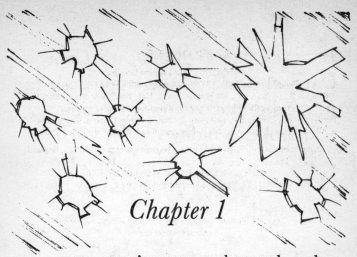

Chapter 1

THE SECRETARY'S VOICE wheezed and clanked through the ancient office intercom. "General Snood? Doctor Greenhorn to see you, sir."

"Send him in," bellowed the General. (He bellowed practically everything.)

With a mighty swipe of his golf club, General Alexander Snood of Cape Catapult Space Centre sent yet another ball crashing through the office window. Snood spent much of his day practising his golf swing, and the window was colandered with holes.

But the General didn't care. Cape Catapult was his little empire. He ran it. He didn't have to worry about the odd broken window.

Besides, it wasn't his office. He was just borrowing it while his was being decorated.

Doctor Axel Greenhorn stepped into
the office just as another ball shot
through the window. Outside there was
a screech of tyres and a muffled crunch
of impact.

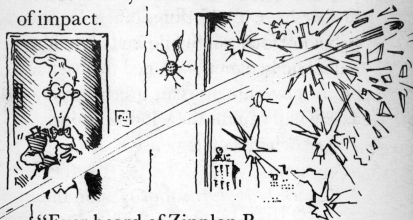

"Ever heard of Zipplon B,
Greenhorn?" the General bellowed.

"I . . . er . . ."

"Of course you haven't – it's Top
Secret!" the General guffawed, and
slapped Greenhorn so heartily on the
back that the doctor had to catch his
glasses before they shot off his nose and
in among the pot plants. "Zipplon B,"

3

the General continued, "is the latest, and probably greatest fuel in space travel. It will send a spaceship twice as far, three times as fast as any fuel we have used before."

Swoof! General Snood belted another ball. The two men flattened themselves on the government issue green carpet, as the ball caught the window frame and ricocheted off expensive equipment.

"Come here, Greenhorn," said the General, clambering up, and walking to the window. Crunching over broken glass, Greenhorn followed.

Cape Catapult Space Centre lay below them in the sunlight. Looking out across the golfball-littered car park, Greenhorn could see the low cluster of hangars, huts and offices. He could even see his own department, the Food

(Artificial) Testing and Selection
Office, or F(A)TSO for short. And
towering above all this was the vast,
gleaming body of the ARK 1 space
shuttle.

"What has all this got to do with
me?" thought Greenhorn. "I don't have

anything to do with the rockets . . .
worse luck!'' Greenhorn probably had
the most boring job in the whole Space
Centre. F(A)TSO was housed in a
rickety old shed on the outskirts of Cape
Catapult. There were fifteen in the
department altogether: Greenhorn . . .
and fourteen animals in cages.

Everyday, scientists from the Section
for Production of Artificial Meals
(SPAM) would send Greenhorn little
plastic packets of fudge-coloured
artificial food, which he would feed to
the animals. Greenhorn
would then watch.
If the animals liked
the food, he would
put ticks on forms
outside the cages.
If it made them ill,
he put crosses.

It was a tedious, tedious job, and Greenhorn HATED it!! If only he could get a job in the centre of things. If only he could work at Mission Control! If only he . . .

"Greenhorn?" The General's voice pulled the doctor out of his daydream so fast that he gave a yelp. "Greenhorn – I want your animals on that ship. I want to know how living things react to that kind of speed and power."

"But General," Greenhorn said, "why not put an astronaut in there?"

Of course it was a good question. The fact was that Snood had already tried to get a human crew for the ARK. And failed. Miserably. It's one thing to have a spacecraft that can travel as fast as a bullet. It's another thing to get someone to sit inside that bullet while you pull the trigger.

General Snood had been to all the best test pilots he knew:

Chuck
Cheezman

Wayne
Manlee

Debbie
Ferelass

But when they heard that the ARK was fast enough to get from here to the moon in the time it takes to sneeze, they all suddenly remembered urgent dentist's appointments, or went to visit relatives in Mongolia. No one, it seemed, wanted to risk going into space so fast that they came back with their head on back to front!

8

Of course, the General didn't tell Doctor Greenhorn all this. All he said to the Doctor was, "I'm in charge of this mission, Greenhorn. And I WANT THOSE ANIMALS!"

As he picked his way through the broken glass and golfballs in the car park, Doctor Greenhorn was deep in thought. This was it! His big chance had arrived. If his animals were in the ARK, then he would have to be at Mission Control . . . where he had

9

always wanted to be! Yahooooo!

There was one small problem. Greenhorn was sending his animals, who trusted him, on a highly dangerous mission. How was he going to tell them? *What* was he going to tell them?

Doctor Axel Greenhorn, though, was a clever man. By the time he reached the F(A)TSO office door, he had decided. He went in and beamed at the animals.

"I have some wonderful news!" he said.

11

Chapter 2

THE NIGHT BEFORE the launch of ARK 1 Doctor Greenhorn was unable to sleep. It wasn't excitement. It was guilt. He stood at his bedroom window, and looked across to where the ARK stood floodlit on the launch pad.

Doctor Greenhorn turned to the one he always turned to in times of trouble. "Einstein," he said, "do you think I did the right thing?" But all he could see reflected in the unblinking eyes of his teddy was his own troubled face.

12

The telephone rang shrilly, and Doctor Greenhorn leapt to pick it up. The unmistakable bellow at the other end said, "We have a pilot. At long last!"

"That's good news, General," the Doctor brightened. "Then you won't need the animals."

"Of course we'll need the animals!"

"But you said you have a pilot."

"We do have a pilot, but he's . . . well, he's a little . . ."

"A little *what*, General?" the Doctor asked.

"You'll see tomorrow!" said the General, and before Greenhorn could ask any more questions:

The line went dead.

Dawn, and the countdown was well under way.

Also well under way was some sort of party in the rear cabin of the ARK. Secure in their specially designed cages, a dozen assorted domestic animals raced each other tunelessly through a song.

The two sheep, Eddie and Silv, seemed to be leading, closely followed by Monty and Charles, the fastidious pig brothers. Blodwyn, a goat, fought for third place with the chickens, while the rats at the back had given up entirely and seemed to be eating the seat stuffing.

As a crack, highly-trained space test pilot, Harvey could bear weightlessness, cold, extremes of temperature, and could survive on water and cardboard for six months, but this row was giving him a headache!

"Can you keep the noise down in the back," he called out. "I can't hear myself think."

"Well really!" huffed the pig brothers.

"Can't you just think louder?" asked the chickens. They didn't catch on very fast.

"Never mind, driver," Blodwyn called. "Only eighteen verses to go!"

Harvey gritted his teeth. He wished they wouldn't keep calling him 'Driver'. Every two minutes since they had been carried into the ARK, these animals had been calling into the front cabin with 'driver' this, and 'driver' that. It was driving him bananas!

BANANAS!! That was it. That was what he had forgotten to pack! Space pilot Harvey chattered and shrieked. He was a genius at maths, spoke twelve languages and knew the complete works of Shakespeare off by heart. Harvey was the most briliiant chimpanzee in the universe, but he never went anywhere without his one little luxury.

"No bananas," muttered Harvey
sulkily. "RATS!"

"Yes? What do you want?"

"Oh, nothing. I was just saying 'rats'."

"Oh," said the rats, and went back to gnawing the seats.

The countdown continued. Shutters slid down over the ARK's windows.

"Are we going now, driver?"

Harvey sighed. "Yes," he said. "We're going now."

10 . . . 9 . . . 8 . . .

Mission Control was tense and quiet. Everyone watched the screen with their fingers crossed. To everyone's surprise, even General Snood was speaking in what was very nearly a whisper. In fact, the General was behaving in a strange way altogether. As he sat gulping coffee and staring at the huge screen, he was practically hidden by a jumble of lucky rabbits, cats, charms, and mascots.

19

3 . . . 2 . . . 1 . . . LIFT OFF!

"Here goes," said Harvey to his passengers.

General Snood was glued to the screen. There was a 'bliff' of smoke, and a ball of white flame, which left purple spots bobbing in front of everyone's eyes. Then, when the smoke had cleared, everybody looked for signs of the ARK.

There were none. The ARK had completely disappeared. Or so it seemed. Then somebody shouted, "Look!" The camera had found the ARK. Already it was a tiny pinpoint of bright light in the early morning sky. Moments later, it had gone again.

"That *is* fast," said Doctor Greenhorn, impressed.

"I wonder," growled General Snood, "if any of them survived the launch."

He didn't wonder long. There was a crackle and hiss from the loudspeaker and then, faint but unmistakable, the sound of voices came over the airwaves . . .

Eight green bottles, hanging on the wall...

Chapter 3

HARVEY STOOD UP, scratched his head, and did a backflip or two to unwind. Then he switched the ARK to automatic pilot, and stepped out of his cabin to see how the animals were getting on.

The animals, as it happened, were getting on fine . . . until they saw Harvey come through the doorway. Then there was a horrendous panic of flapping and bleating and squawks.

"Have you taken leave of your senses, driver!" squealed Monty the pig.

"What are you talking about?"
Harvey demanded.

"You!" cried Blodwyn. "You
shouldn't be back here! You should be
watching the road."

Harvey hooted with laughter. "What
road?" he said.

The animals looked at each other.
Then the window shutters hummed
open. They all looked out across an

endless blue blackness, flecked with blinking stars.

"Well? What did you expect?" said Harvey. "A coach trip?"

There was a moment of embarrassment. Then one of the chickens spoke. "Actually, that's exactly what we expected," she said.

Cape Catapult Space Centre was celebrating a perfect launch. General Snood was dancing around and throwing streamers. Doctor Greenhorn, on the other hand, was quietly dreaming of a glittering future. When the world knew that his animals had been round the galaxy twice, TV and newspaper people would be falling over themselves to talk to him. He'd be famous. A star. A celebrity. His name would be on everyone's lips.

Little did he know that way above him in the ARK, his name was already on everyone's lips.

And what they were saying about him wasn't nice at all!

"A holiday?" Harvey exclaimed, unable to believe his ears.

So that was why they had all been calling him 'driver'. Doctor Greenhorn, the coward, had told his animals that they were going on holiday. No mention of danger. No mention of being shot into space at hundreds of miles per hour. Small wonder the animals were feeling gloomy, thought Harvey. They had been expecting a few days at the seaside! To try and cheer them all up, Harvey said, "Shall I let you out for a while?"

"Don't be daft!" said Blodwyn. "There's no air – we'd all die!"

"Not out of the ship, dimwit. I meant out of the cages."

After pointing out that her name was not Dimwit, Blodwyn politely declined the offer of freedom. She and the other animals were better staying in their cages. "You know where you are when you're in a cage," she said, which struck Harvey as pretty obvious – of course you knew where you were. You were in a cage!

"But wouldn't you like to stretch your legs?"

Blodwyn shook her head. "We are scientific pioneers," she said loftily. "We were put into cages to serve the cause of science. We should be proud to stay in them!"

"I have never heard so much rot in all my life. Who told you that?" asked Harvey.

Blodwyn thought for a moment. "Er . . . Doctor Greenhorn," she said finally.

"Oh," said Harvey. "You mean the man who told you that you were going on a seaside holiday?"

The animals all looked at each other, then at Blodwyn, and then at Harvey.

"Perhaps," Blodwyn said, "perhaps we will just pop out for a while, after all."

Harvey went to fetch the keys.

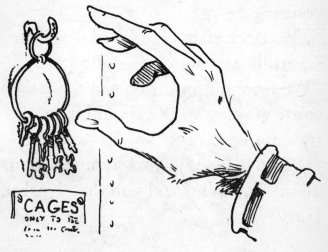

CAGES
ONLY TO BE

As time passed, life on board the ARK improved a lot. While the ship bleeped around the edge of the galaxy, Harvey began to tell the animals about what they were missing. He talked about farms, and open air, and grass, and trees. Blodwyn and the others had never heard of any of these things, but the more they heard, the more they liked the sound of them. In a couple of days they were chanting things like:

We want to get mucky and eat <u>swill</u> !

Harvey was very happy that the animals had cheered up, until he suddenly realised that he had started something that he couldn't finish! After all, he didn't have a farm. When they

29

got back to Earth, Harvey would go back to being the first fully-trained space cadet chimp and Blodwyn and Co would go straight back to Doctor Greenhorn, and F(A)TSO, whether they liked it or not!

He was still thinking through this problem at about nine o'clock on the third day, when something happened that changed EVERYTHING!

Chapter 4

THEY WERE JUST bringing the
sandwiches round at Mission Control,
when a large blip appeared on the
radar, right behind the ARK. A hubbub
of voices broke out. General Snood
went white. Doctor Greenhorn stopped
and stared, a sandwich halfway to his
mouth.

"What is *that*?" he gasped.

The sandwich man looked down. "I
think it's egg-and-cress, sir," he said.

"Not *that*!" Greenhorn jabbed a
finger at the screen. "THAT!"

31

"Looks like a meteor to me, sir – big one too!"

General Snood started to gibber. "Nooooo," he sobbed. "Nonononono!!"

And at that moment, the two blips collided.

There was a stunned silence at Mission Control, Cape Catapult. They scanned the radar screens. They listened for tell-tale bleeps . . . but there was nothing!

"We've lost them, General," someone said.

The great General Snood shook his head. "Not again," he mumbled, "not again!"

It was supposed to be a private mutter, but Doctor Greenhorn heard it. "What do you mean, 'Not again!'? Has this happened before?"

General Snood shuffled awkwardly in

his seat, like a guilty schoolboy. Checking to make sure no one else was listening, he whispered to Greenhorn, "It was years ago. I was about your age. We had just launched a moon mission when POWEEE! Exactly the same thing. Some coincidence, huh?"

"This 'other time'," said the doctor, "was anyone on board?"

Snood nodded gravely. "One of our best space mechanics," he groaned. "Name of Crust. Ozalid Crust." Turning away suddenly to wipe his nose, the General bellowed, "ANY SIGN OF THEM?"

But there was no sign at all. The ARK had disappeared from the radar screen, leaving no blip, no sound. No clue at all. It was as if the ARK had never existed; and certainly, everyone agreed that nothing could have survived a crash like that . . .

Admittedly, for the members of ARK 1 the arrival of the meteor was a surprise.

There was just a **WHOOOSH!**

and a **CRASH!**

and then everything turned

over   and   over   and   over.

"ROAD HOG," squealed Monty, which was strange coming from a pig. "Did you get his number, Harvey?"

Harvey did not reply. He stayed very calm and scratched his head. Then, with incredible speed he did this sum in his head.

$$N = \frac{X}{32,000,00} = 4 \sqrt[4]{75,000}$$

$$(E = MC^4 \times 3.45) \times 4\sqrt{\quad} \quad 42^{10}$$

$$284 \times (4)^2 = \frac{95.8}{} + 12 \times (3.01)$$

$$VEL = M \times 322,000,000,000$$

$$42^{10} = ADC \times 4r^2 \div 3.721.$$

At the same time, he pushed, flicked, and twiddled controls. The ARK began to slow down in its tumbling, and finally, they were steady once more. A bit shaky perhaps, but otherwise fine. The rats looked a bit off-colour, but everyone said it served them right for

36

eating their seats (at one sitting, as it were).

The animals cheered and clapped enthusiastically. "Well done, Harvey!" they called to their grinning hero. "You were brilliant!"

Only Blodwyn asked quietly, "Where are we?"

Harvey looked out of the window and tried to find familiar stars and planets in order to pinpoint their position. Then he turned, and said, with absolute certainty,

I have no idea!

Chapter 5

THE CHICKENS WERE beginning to
wonder if Harvey was quite all right.
For some time now he had been still
and silent. Apart from scratching his
head occasionally, their pilot seemed
to do nothing but stare into space.
(And there was a lot of it to stare
into!)

"What's he doing, Blod?" they asked.

"Thinking," Blodwyn replied.

The chickens fell silent. They were
wondering what thinking was.

Harvey was still for so long that when

38

he finally looked round, all the animals jumped.

"I think I've worked out what happened," he said when they had all landed in their seats again. "That meteor must have knocked us into another galaxy."

"Wow," murmured the rats.

"Another galaxy?" gasped Eddie and Silv.

"What meteor?" asked the chickens, who didn't catch on very fast.

Blodwyn was just about to run over recent events, very slowly, for the benefit of the chickens, when Silv said, "Loooooook!"

Everybody turned.

Everybody looked.

Everybody took a deep breath and said YEUUUUUUUUUGH!

It was a planet. Sort of.

Imagine you took an enormous pile of old tins, rusty cars, buckled wheels, junk of every shape, size and

description – but all the same brown colour. Imagine you then added old polystyrene boxes and plastic bags of mouldy bread. Suppose you took all that, rolled it into a ball, held it together with wire and a greenish-brown sludge, and hung it in the middle of space.

Well, that's the kind of planet we're talking about!

It was the dirtiest, ugliest, rustbucketiest planet Harvey had ever seen. But he'd have to land there, to see whether the meteor had caused any serious damage to the outside of the ARK.

Harvey swung the ship round and headed for the flattest bit of the planet he could find. Then using his skill and lightning reflexes, he brought the ARK in for a perfect landing.

Well, . . . *almost* perfect!

"According to my tests," said Harvey as the ARK's door slid open, "the air is breathable."

They all filled their lungs . . . and then wished they hadn't. Spluttering and coughing, the **ARK Company** learnt a lesson – just because air is breathable, that doesn't mean that it's *nice* to breathe!

Harvey and the animals picked their way as best they could over the

42

landscape of twisted metal and rubbish, and slimy plastic and other things that they weren't at all sure they wanted to recognise. Slowly, they made their way to a little raised, nearly flat portion. Silv kept getting her wool caught in jagged bits of wire, but apart from that they arrived safely on the 'island'.

"What a dump!" said the rats. Which just about summed it up for everyone.

"Hello, what's this?" said Harvey. Half-buried in the rubbish was an old sign. Pulling it out, Harvey read:

"That must be a very old sign," Harvey muttered.

"How do you know that?" said the chickens, who didn't catch on very fast.

"Because this hasn't been a paradise planet for years."

"And I think I know why," said Blodwyn. "Look."

It was another sign. This one read:

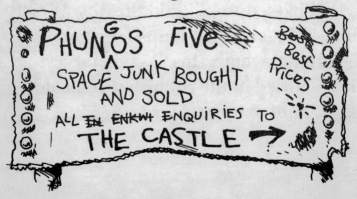

They looked beyond the sign. Rising, tottering above the slurry and litter was a hideous kind of building, made up of fungus and dust, rubble and junk, mouldy cardboard and rotten wood. A long, lumpy drive led through a gateway of rusty iron sheet. The words 'THE CASTLE' were daubed across this gate in dripping, grey-green paint.

"You know," said Monty, "I have a terrible feeling someone actually lives up there."

"Someone," muttered Harvey, "or some*thing*!"

A voice boomed through the castle. "Derv? Where are you?"

Deep in the innards of the building, a strange figure squeaked and skittered along grubby passages and litter-filled corridors. It was made up of all sorts of things; a bit of radio here, a roller-skate spare part there. The body itself was made from an old petrol pump, and across its front, you could still make out the word 'DERV'.

Rounding a final corner, Derv arrived in the main hall, at the end of which, the owner of the booming voice stood muttering over a battered TV.

He was a big man, and what hair he had stuck out in all directions. He wore an ancient, dusty overcoat on top of at least three layers of cardigans and woollies. Something seemed to be wrong with the TV. The rolling picture made it look like a tumble-drier, and every so often the man would thump the top, and growl when there was no improvement. Ozalid Crust, astronaut, space mechanic, and master of Crust Castle was clueless about televisions.

"Flippin' thing's on the blink again," he muttered. "What's wrong with it, Derv?"

Derv's computer brain clicked into action. Then, with a voice like a radio in a bucket, Derv gave his report. "The television aerial has been knocked by a UFO which has just landed, sir."

"A WHAT?" stormed Crust.

"A UFO, sir. An unidentified flying ob–"

"I know what it stands for!" Ozalid Crust snapped grumpily. "Why wasn't I told about it?"

Derv quaked, and little loose bits rattled about inside him. "I was just coming to tell you, sir, when you . . . er . . . called me."

Crust glowered at his mechanical butler. "Go and find this UFO, and see if it's got a captain. Find out all about it. I want to know what it's doing on *my* planet, flying past *my* castle, messing with *my* telly aerial!" Derv reversed a few feet. "And bring whoever's in charge to me." For the first time that day, he smiled. "I'll get my SCARY clothes on!"

Derv sped across the floor. He had just reached the hall door, when the voice of Ozalid Crust stopped him in his tracks. "By the way," he said. "Find out if he can do TV repairs."

Chapter 6

HARVEY SCRATCHED HIS head and frowned at the huge dents in the side of the ARK. They actually looked much worse than they were, but all the same,

his radio-receiving equipment was badly mangled. It would take a day or so to fix it. Then he must try and get back to Earth.

The animals looked miserably around their temporary home. As a first taste of freedom it was nothing to write home about. And on top of everything else, they were getting HUNGRY!

Blodwyn turned to Monty and Charles. "Say what you like about Greenhorn. He always came round to feed us. As regular as clockwork!"

The pig brothers nodded, stomachs rumbling. "We're starving," they moaned.

"There's nothing to eat round here," Silv and Eddie said, looking with wrinkled-up noses at the surrounding junk. Even the rats agreed, and they would eat almost *anything*. One of the chickens looked up. "I could do you eggs," she said.

The animals were too busy complaining to hear Derv, as he trundled daintily across the tip towards them. "Ahem," he said.

With a squawking and flapping that would have deafened Old Macdonald, the animals shot down holes and behind drums to hide. Not Harvey, though. Harvey was highly trained. He had seen too much of life to be impressed by a petrol pump. Even a red, rolling one that could tap him on the shoulder and say, "Excuse me, but are you in charge?"

Well, all right – he was a little bit impressed. He stayed calm though, as always, and simply nodded.

"Then I wonder," Derv said, "if you would mind stepping this way?"

Harvey turned to the animals, who were just beginning to show their faces again. "Wait for me here for ten minutes!" he said. "If I'm not back by then . . . er . . . wait for another ten minutes!"

Blodwyn leapt from her hiding place. "Hold on! What about us?" she bleated.

"What about food?" the rats squealed. "We're starving!"

"Why didn't you say so?" Harvey cried. "Help yourselves. It's in the front cabin, second drawer down, next to the one marked 'socks'. Blodwyn's in charge of rations." He turned to Derv. "Right," he said, "take me to your leader!"

Derv swung wildly round, and began to bowl along towards the castle. Harvey shrugged, and followed.

It had been some time since Phungos 5 had had visitors, and Derv was making the most of it. He talked. And talked. And talked. Was this Harvey's first time on the planet, he asked, and had they come far, and how long had he been an astronaut, and Ooooreally?

was he from Earth-well-of-course-I've-
never-been-there-myself-but-I-hear-
it's-nice, and were they his animals,
and wasn't the weather awful well of
course we've had the best of it, and
did Harvey know anything about TV
and . . .

Harvey sighed. If this was how petrol
pumps talked, he decided, he was going
to avoid them in future.

They had reached the castle gate.
Derv pointed up the uneven drive. "Up
there, through the arch, first right, past
the bins, and it's the double doors at the
end. Have a nice day." Then, with a

twirl, a clank, and a whizz, he shot around a corner, and was gone.

Harvey waited until the squeaking had faded away in the distance. Then he stepped forward. The first thing Harvey noticed about Crust Castle was the smell. Even the flies were holding their noses. It was hard to tell exactly what smell it was . . . It was a mixture – old chips, old hamburgers, old socks, old teabags . . . old EVERYTHING!

Bits of stuff lay everywhere: wodges of wet newspaper, lumps of food with green fuzz on them. Then there were bits of bikes, bits of computers, bits of boxes and boxes of bits – all piled on every side.

As Harvey got closer he noticed something else too. Crust Castle was just hanging together. It actually creaked, and swayed slightly in the breeze.

Following Derv's instructions as best he could, Harvey made his way into the Castle. He did try to ask directions from a lamppost, but it turned out to be *just* a lamppost . . . either that, or it was ignoring him! Finally though, he found himself outside the double doors. He took a deep breath.

And pushed.

He was standing at one end of an

enormous hall. Flies flitted and
hummed in the light that seeped
through cracks in the walls, which
seemed to be composed of bits
of old spaceship, and flattened
oildrums.

Harvey blinked as his eyes adjusted

to what light
there was in
the strange room.
Then, at the top of
some steps at the far end,
he saw a tall, impressive
figure with its back to him.
It was Ozalid Crust.

59

Ozalid Crust was well known in this neck of the nebula, as a space junk-dealer. Every now and again, space travellers from all over the galaxy would drop in to buy spare parts from Ozalid's vast supply. He also did bits of welding and rivetting – for a price – and if your ship was wrecked, he'd buy it from you.

But Ozalid Crust was not content to be a scrap-dealer. He wanted to be a powerful and ruthless space ruler – just like the ones in all the films he watched on TV. He dreamed of being a big, frightening character: a character who would strike fear into the hearts of the people who came to buy or sell their junk.

So one day, Ozalid Crust had sat down and designed a Space Baddy Costume. And this was what he wore, as he slowly turned to glare at Harvey.

"Approach!" he snarled.

Harvey was bemused by this strange
figure. Whoever it was that stood there,

seemed to be dressed in an assortment
of plastic bottles and food containers.
These had been cut roughly in half,
painted silver, and attached to old
woolly tights. Ozalid also had on an old
blanket cloak, and carried menacingly
in his hand a 'space blaster gun'. (It
looked to Harvey suspiciously like
something you might spray greenfly
with!) Harvey was not so much
frightened as worried – worried that the
whole ridiculous costume would fall
apart as soon as his host tried to walk!

Harvey reached the bottom of the
steps, and looked up.

Then the strange figure spoke, or
rather boomed, in a voice that made
the walls rattle and vibrate. "So you
dare to bring your puny craft onto *my*
planet."

"Keep your hair on," said Harvey.

"There's no need to shout. I'm not deaf."

Ozalid Crust was a little taken aback. More than a little. "How dare you speak like that to me, snivelling earth creature. Do you know who I am?"

"No, I don't," said Harvey simply.

Ozalid Crust took a step backwards. This wasn't going to plan at all. He was in his best Space Baddy Clothes, with his most terrifying voice making his throat sore already. All this usually scared people silly. By now Harvey should have been shaking, and terrified. Or begging for mercy. Preferably all three. But he wasn't. He was standing there, scratching his head. Perhaps I'm not shouting loudly enough, thought Ozalid to himself. He took a deep breath, and BELLOWED!

"I AM OZALID CRUST!!" He

began to stride down the steps. "I AM
RULER OF PHUNGOS 5. I AM THE
MASTER OF THE PLANET. I AM
EEEEEeeeeeeeeeep!!"

His voice rose to a hamsterish squeal as
his cloak caught on a nail. "I am
s-stuck!" he squeaked, heaving at the
threadbare material. "I'll be (tug) with
you (tug) in a . . ."

With one last, desperate yank,
accompanied by a long RRRRRRRIIIP!,
the cloak came suddenly free. Ozalid
gawped like a goldfish as he tried, and

failed, to keep his balance. Clattering and rolling down the steps like a runaway kitchen utensil, he finally came to rest at the feet of his 'victim'. Bits of leg armour had found their way onto his head, making it difficult to see. He shook them off . . . and stared. "You look like a monkey," he said.

If Harvey was impressed by this display of brainpower, he didn't show it. Looking down at Ozalid Crust, he said, "And you look like a buffoon."

Ozalid leapt up, speechless with rage. Nobody had ever called him a buffoon before. He wasn't even sure what a buffoon *was*, but he was pretty sure that it wasn't nice!

"What's the matter?" he demanded crossly, feeling his fearsomeness fritter away. "Aren't you frightened?"

"No. Aren't you?" Harvey looked at him. "If I were you I'd be terrified of breaking my neck, dressed like that!"

Ozalid Crust was feeling more and more foolish. "Look, what do you want?" he demanded sulkily. "What are you doing on my planet?"

Harvey explained that the ARK had crash-landed on Phungos 5, and that what he and his friends wanted more than anything was to get straight back off it! All Harvey needed was some spare parts.

At the sound of 'spare parts' Ozalid Crust transformed. He smiled; he rubbed his hands together. "Why didn't you say so? I can help you there. I've got spare parts. Loads of 'em. This whole planet's full of spare parts."

"I know it is," said Harvey. "I've seen it. It's an absolute disgrace!"

The smile fell off Ozalid's face. "WHAT!"

"You heard me," Harvey continued. "You've let this planet go to pot!"

"Listen, sonny," said Ozalid airily, absentmindedly flicking crumbs off his cloak. "When I came to this planet I had nothing . . . NOTHING! My spaceship crash-landed, just like yours, and *I* didn't have," with a sweep of his arm, he indicated the Castle, "a lovely cosy place to go for help. All I had was a pile of junk, and this." He tapped his

67

head. "I put up my sign, and I waited. They all started to come here – space pirates, space traders, everyone. Selling their junk . . . buying mine. You name it. I've sold it. Or bought it. One or the other. And look at me now."

"I am," said Harvey. "And all I can see is a lazy, careless, slovenly layabout, who's turned a beautiful place into a rubbish tip! You should be ashamed of yourself."

Chapter 7

DERV WAS IN the servant's cellar, untangling some string from his castors, when he heard the roaring voice of his master. He scooted down the corridors, and burst into the hall. He was just in time to see Ozalid Crust trying to shoo Harvey out with a metal detector. Harvey, meanwhile, was screeching and chattering, and flip-flapping from floor to walls, walls to steps, steps to lamps. Several times he bounded, somersaulting over Ozalid himself. Every time Crust took a swing at where

Harvey had been, Harvey wasn't there any more! Instead, Ozalid's swinging detector would whack a plate, or a pole out of its place in the wall. The hall was already littered with broken-off pieces and Derv could see more

daylight than usual through newly-knocked holes.

"SLOVENLY??" Ozalid was roaring. "I'll give you slovenly." Again the metal detector connected with a piece of wall, and something like a hub-cap went clattering across the floor.

"You are slovenly," Harvey yelled from the safety of a wall bracket. "You've let every Tom, Dick and Harry leave their space junk here, until what used to be a paradise planet is floating around like a dustbin in orbit."

"Rubbish," snorted Ozalid.

"Exactly. Tons of it. You've ruined a perfectly nice planet!"

"I haven't."

"You have."

Ozalid spied his mechanical butler at the door. "Derv. This planet isn't ruined, is it?"

Derv shuffled from wheel to wheel. "Well, actually . . . sir . . . um . . ."

"Well?" Ozalid Crust tapped his foot impatiently.

Derv looked from his boss, to Harvey and back again. Then he trundled slowly to where a new and gaping hole

72

gave a pretty good view of Phungos. "Perhaps Sir would like to see for himself," he said.

Ozalid Crust looked out on his planet for the first time in years. His eyebrows went up so high, Harvey thought they might go right over his head, and drop off the other side. The amateur Space Baddy tried hard to think of something to say, but the best he could come up with was . . . "Oh."

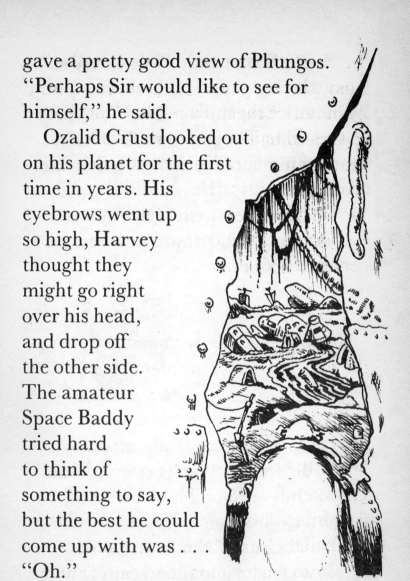

"See?" Harvey said. "You were so busy playing games up here, you didn't even notice the mess pile up."

Ozalid had begun to sniff. Derv handed him a rag and the big man blew his nose loudly. "How did it happen, Derv?" he asked, genuinely confused.

Derv sat Ozalid down, and began to unfold the story.

It had all started, really, with the TV. "Before my time, of course," said Derv, "but Sir found it on an old space freighter, I believe."

Ozalid Crust nodded miserably.

"It was just a monitor, really, but for

some reason, you could get Earth
Television pictures on it. That was
when Sir decided to build me, and a few
other service robots, to run the junk
business for him. We would sort
through the rubbish, and do the
mending and welding, while the
customers came up here –"

"To meet the 'Master of the
Universe'?" sighed Harvey.

Ozalid looked up. "But why didn't
you tell me about . . . that?" he asked,
jerking his head in the direction of the
window.

"I tried sir," said Derv, "really I did.
Several times. But you were usually
watching a space film . . ."

Ozalid shuffled sadly across and
looked again at the mess he had made
of the planet. He shook his head and
leaned against the wall.

SKEEEEEEEEEEEEEK!

High up in the roof of the jerry-built Castle there was a sound – just as if fingernails had been scraped down a blackboard, but much, much louder. Ozalid, Harvey and Derv all heard it. Way over at the ARK, the animals heard it, puzzled, shrugged, and got on with their food.

Back in the castle,
Ozalid felt the
wall shudder and
twang as, with a
series of clatters,
rusty, dusty little
bits of tin and
plastic began to
skitter down and
patter in the dust
on the floor.
Along one of
the wall seams,
there was a
drum-roll of
metallic pops
as rivets unzipped
themselves.

Harvey was
the first to realise
what was happening. In his fury earlier,

Ozalid had knocked so many bits out of the castle wall that the whole fragile building was about to give way. A long split of daylight appeared in the wall next to them and shot upward at alarming speed.

"Run," Harvey shouted.

"No," Ozalid sobbed. "I can't run, I'm much too upset."

"You'll get flattened if you stay here!"

"Well, all right then I'll run. But mind you don't go too fast. I'm not as young as I was."

Derv zipped in front of him and wheeled round. "Climb on my back, your Crustiness. I'll do the rest."

Harvey scampered out through the door with Derv in hot pursuit, wheels screeching as he swerved to avoid a rain of pipes and girders. Ozalid Crust clung on. Eyes tight closed, with bits falling off his silly costume, he tried not to whimper.

The three of them careered out of the gates at full pelt, to be joined by the lamppost. (So he was ignoring me, thought Harvey). They stopped, the machines steaming, Ozalid and Harvey wheezing, and looked back.

The castle leaned slowly one way, then the other, with pieces falling everywhere. Then with a screeching, tearing sound, like an orchestra being torn apart, it seemed to buckle, sit down and collapse slowly sideways in a cloud of greeny-grey dust. Ozalid sniffed, and a tear plinked onto his plastic armour.

"My telly," was all he said.

No one spoke for a little while. They just watched as the dust settled on the ruins of Ozalid's castle. All that was left was the gate, creaking slightly in the breeze.

Then, suddenly, there was an

81

almighty noise, as the ARK animals all came bounding, flapping and strutting across the tip, shouting, "What happened, Harvey," and "Are you all right?" and "Who's this?" all at once.

In the middle of this cacophany, there was a sudden cry of joy from, of all people, Ozalid Crust!

"Animals," he gasped. Grinning broadly, he wagged his finger at Harvey. "You never told me you had *animals*. I *love* animals."

"Love animals?" Harvey said. Surely his ears were playing tricks. "How come?"

"Well," said Ozalid, beaming, "when there were no space films on telly, I used to tune in to farming programmes. I like farming programmes. I used to think I'd either like to be a farmer, or a space baddy. And of course there were no animals on Phungos 5, so farming was right out, until now." He looked at the animals longingly. Then with a sad sniff, he continued. "But I suppose you'll be going back to Earth as soon as your ship is fixed, and I'll be left all on my own again." Taking the hanky that the faithful Derv had produced from somewhere, Ozalid blew his nose noisily.

"Wait a minute," Blodwyn said. "I don't know about the others, but I for one don't want to go back to F(A)TSO." There were mutterings of agreement. "As far as we're concerned, Doctor Greenhorn can keep his cages AND his yukky food, so if you've got a better offer, Mr Crust, we'd like to hear it!"

Harvey gently pushed Ozalid Crust forward. The Ex-Evil Overlord of

Phungos 5 cleared his throat. If the animals would stay with him on Phungos 5, he said, he would clear up the planet personally, and build a farm. He would look after the animals. In return they would give him eggs, milk, cheese and wool. The pigs would keep things tidy. And he'd leave a very small rubbish tip for the rats to play in.

"Well?" he asked nervously when he had finished.

"One moment please," said Blodwyn. "I have to discuss your offer with my friends!" The animals went into a huddle. There were whispers and grunts. Ozalid Crust crossed his fingers. Then Blodwyn finally stepped up.

"Mr Crust," she said. "My members have taken a vote. It's a deal! You have a farm!"

* * * * * * * * *

Derv watched as Ozalid Crust put the
final touches to his farmhouse. It was a
little odd-looking, made up as it was
from bits of a shuttle that had reversed
into an asteroid, but Ozalid had made
it homely enough. Derv had never seen
his master looking so fit, or working so
hard. In a matter of days he had
transformed the little planet, and grass
was already sprouting where he had
cleared the junk away into neat piles.

85

"He's like a new man," said Derv, turning to Harvey. "He's up at the crack of dawn every day, clearing away more junk. He really does enjoy the outdoor life."

"More than he enjoyed being a space baddy?" asked Harvey.

"Much more," said Derv. "I mean, let's face it, he was never a very *good* baddy, was he?" They both chuckled.

"I propose a toast," Harvey said, raising his glass of lemonade. "To Ozalid Crust!"

"No," said Derv. "To *FARMER* Crust. Farmer Crust of Phungos 5!"

"I'll drink to that!" said Harvey.

And he did.

A sign on the front gate announced to the World that Cape Catapult Space Centre was 'UNDER NEW MANAGEMENT'.

A new General was in charge of a new project, and the new ARK 2 shuttle stood on the launch pad as the seconds ticked away. Inside, the two test pilots turned to each other.

"Good luck," said Pilot General Snood, hoping his co-pilot wouldn't see him cross his fingers.

"Same to you," said Pilot Doctor Greenhorn, hoping the General wouldn't see him crossing *his* fingers.

The two men gulped, and waited for . . .

Some other Young Puffin Story Books

ALLOTMENT LANE IN LONDON
Margaret Joy

No one in Miss Mee's class has ever been to London before, so everybody is really excited about this term's school trip. With a boat trip on the river, visits to a market, museums and the zoo, and even an unexpected lesson in rhyming slang, there's a lot to fit in to four days. So keep together everyone, and don't get lost! The children from Allotment Lane School have great fun (and a few frights) in this entertaining collection of stories.

THE SQUIRREL WIFE
Philippa Pearce

Jack's reward for rescuing one of the Green People is a gold ring, and the promise of a wife – a beautiful squirrel-wife, who will teach him the secrets of the forest. So begin Jack's strange adventures in a world of mystery and enchantment. Here is an original fairy tale to live in the imagination of any child, as timeless as the ancient forest itself.

JEFFREY'S JOKE MACHINE
Alexander McCall Smith

Everyone likes a good laugh, and Jeffrey can't believe his luck when he finds an old joke machine which really works. Soon people are queuing up for their very own joke, and laughing till they cry. But then something goes badly wrong – has the joke machine lost its sense of humour? Or could it have something to do with bad-tempered Mr Jenkinson, who lost his years ago?

THE RED SECRET
Jenny Nimmo

When the Turner family leaves London to live in a small village in Shropshire, Tom and his sister Daisy feel very left out. The village children are suspicious of them and are reluctant to make friends. However, when he is given a strange present by a boy in his class, Tom is drawn into an adventure which results in acceptance and new friends for both himself and Daisy.

BONESHAKER
Paul and Emma Rogers

She's old, a bit dusty and a bit rusty, but Oliver knows she's a very special bicycle. For Boneshaker has a mind of her own. With a bike like her, life's bound to be exciting, and these four stories are full of races, rescues and breathtaking rides!

THE INTERGALACTIC KITCHEN
Frank Rodgers

When the red light on Mr Bird's safety and protection system signals a class 1A emergency, Mrs Bird and her children follow the instructions. To their amazement they blast off into space in their kitchen.

The family's adventures in their intergalactic kitchen are told using a wonderful mix of text and comic strip, making this story fantastic fun to read.

SEARCH FOR THE SAUCY SALLY
Tony Bradman

Left with nothing after a shopping spree on Market Island, the Bluebeards are determined to find their ship, The Saucy Sally. But when they are shipwrecked in shark-infested waters, it looks like time is fast running out.

CONTEST AT CUTLASS COVE
Tony Bradman

The Bluebeard family are determined to win the Pirates of the Year contest for the fourth time. So they can't believe their bad luck when one thing after another goes disastrously wrong for them – and mysteriously right for the unfit Bulger family.

A MEDAL FOR MALINA
Narinda Dhami

Malina is a fast runner and she knows she can beat any other girl in the school. But can she beat John 'Bigmouth' Parry, with his boasting about how great *he* is, and how stupid girls are? Doesn't everyone know that girls can never run as fast as boys?

Sports day is coming and neither John nor Malina can resist the challenge. And in this exciting story the day of the big race arrives in a thrilling climax.